KILLER SNAKES

Russell Freedman

HOLIDAY HOUSE

New York

To KATE, who asked for this book

Copyright © 1982 by Russell Freedman
All rights reserved
Printed in the United States of America
First Edition

Library of Congress Cataloging in Publication Data

Freedman, Russell.
Killer snakes.

Includes index.
Summary: Photographs and text introduce some
deadly snakes and describe the ways they kill.
1. Poisonous snakes—Juvenile literature.
[1. Poisonous snakes. 2. Snakes] I. Title.
QL666.06F84   597.96   82-80821
ISBN 0-8234-0460-9   AACR2

Burmese python (title page)
JESSIE COHEN/OFFICE OF
GRAPHICS AND EXHIBITS,
NATIONAL ZOOLOGICAL PARK,
SMITHSONIAN INSTITUTION

Contents

The head of a cobra, one of the world's most dangerous snakes
EDWARD S. ROSS/CALIFORNIA ACADEMY OF SCIENCES

How Snakes Stay Alive

All snakes are hunters. They stay alive by killing and eating other animals. Mostly they eat animals like mice, rats, lizards, birds, and smaller snakes. From the moment a snake is born, it knows how to hunt for its food.

When a snake hunts, it must strike quickly. It has no arms to help it grab and hold its prey. Some snakes catch their prey by coiling their bodies around them. Some hang on with their sharp teeth. And some kill their prey with a poisonous bite.

Of the 2,700 kinds of snakes in the world, only 412 kinds are poisonous. About half of these are too small to be a real threat to people.

A poisonous snake stays away from people whenever it can. It needs its poison for hunting. If it is in danger, it will try to hide or escape. But if it can't get away, then it may bite. When people are bitten, it is usually because they step on a snake, get too close, or try to pick one up.

This book describes some of the world's deadliest snakes. Most of them are poisonous, but two kinds are not. They are the giant pythons (PIE-thons) and anacondas (an-uh-KON-duhs).

Giant Constrictors

Pythons and anacondas are the world's biggest snakes. The largest python ever found was 33 feet long. The biggest anaconda was 37 feet long. If such a snake climbed up the side of a three-story house, its head would reach the roof before its tail left the ground.

Pythons and anacondas are not poisonous. They are giant constrictors (kun-STRIK-turs). They kill their prey by coiling around them and squeezing. They do not crush their victims' bones, as many people think. Instead, they squeeze until the victim stops breathing. It takes just a few minutes for a giant constrictor to kill a goat or a deer.

Anacondas live in the steamy jungles of northern South America. They lurk near swamps and rivers, where they prey on animals that come to drink. Like all snakes, they swallow their victims whole. One anaconda swallowed a six-foot alligator. After a meal like that, an anaconda can go for months without eating.

Giant anaconda

Pythons live in the jungles of Africa and southern Asia. Like anacondas, they are expert swimmers. They also climb trees with ease.

Some pythons are only a few feet long. They can be quite friendly and have been kept as pets. Other pythons are too big to handle. The giants include the Indian python (up to 20 feet), the African python (up to 25 feet), and the regal python (up to 33 feet).

Giant pythons can swallow some very large animals. An Indian python once swallowed a deer that had 12-inch horns. A regal python killed and swallowed a leopard. Another regal python swallowed a black bear that weighed about 200 pounds.

If giant pythons and anacondas were common, they would be a real menace. But they're not. Since they live deep in the jungle, they seldom meet people. Attacks on humans are rare. These snakes can kill a person, but they're not as dangerous as many poisonous snakes that are much smaller.

Indian python

Cobras and Their Relatives

Cobras live in many parts of Africa and Asia. They crawl through fields, hunting for rats and mice to eat. They hide near houses, where people can step on them at night. In India, cobras kill as many as 10,000 people every year.

When taken by surprise, a cobra may strike suddenly. But if given a chance, it will warn an enemy to get away. It hisses loudly, rears up, and spreads its neck into a "hood." Then it sways back and forth as it measures the distance to its target. If the enemy doesn't back away, the cobra strikes.

Like other poisonous snakes, a cobra has two sharp fangs at the top of its mouth. Each fang is connected to a poison gland in its cheeks. When the cobra bites, muscles in its cheeks squeeze against the poison glands. Poison flows down a tube in each fang. It squirts through a tiny hole at the tip of the fang and enters the victim's wound.

Cobra skull
T. BIERWERT/COURTESY
AMERICAN MUSEUM OF
NATURAL HISTORY

Indian cobra ready to strike. These cobras reach a length of about 6 feet.

Red spitting cobra
LOS ANGELES ZOO

Some cobras spit their poison at an enemy. In place of tiny holes at the tips of their fangs, they have holes in front of each fang. When they squirt poison, it shoots forward into the air. A cobra can spit its poison as far as 8 feet. And it usually hits its target.

Before firing, a spitting cobra holds its head very still. It opens its jaws slightly. Then it lets go with two swift jets of yellow poison. Some cobras can spit several times in a row. They seem to aim at the eyes of their enemies. Their poison makes the eyes sting and burn, giving the cobra a chance to escape. If the poison isn't washed out right away, it can injure the eyes and even cause blindness. Zoo workers who handle these snakes must wear face masks to protect their eyes.

A cobra spits only to protect itself. To kill an animal, it must actually bite and squirt poison into the wound.

A king cobra can be 18 feet long. It's the biggest poisonous snake in the world. It is also one of the most fearless. It will attack an elephant.

One of these snakes carries enough poison to kill as many as 120 people. Luckily, king cobras do not attack people often. They live in the wilderness, away from farms and villages.

The king cobra is one of the few snakes to guard its eggs. The female builds a nest by scraping leaves together into a big mound. She lays as many as fifty eggs in the middle of it. Then she coils up and guards the eggs until they hatch. She will attack anyone who comes close to her hidden nest.

A baby cobra is ready for action as soon as it hatches. Even before it leaves its egg, it begins to rear up and spread its hood. Drop for drop, its poison is as deadly as its parents'.

*King cobra guarding her eggs
at the Bronx Zoo in New York*
© NEW YORK ZOOLOGICAL SOCIETY

King cobra hatching
© NEW YORK ZOOLOGICAL SOCIETY

Kraits (krites) are found only in Southeast Asia. During the day they are sleepy and timid. But at night, when they prowl for food, they are much bolder. They become a real danger to any barefoot person walking along a trail.

In India, the common krait is called the "seven-stepper." The Indians say that if a krait bites you, you have time for only seven steps before dying. Actually, no snake has a poison that works so fast. And yet the nickname shows how much the Indians fear these deadly snakes.

No snake in Africa is more dreaded than the black mamba (MOM-buh). It grows to a length of 14 feet. That makes it the second biggest poisonous snake after the king cobra. When a black mamba strikes, it rears up so high that it can reach a person's head.

Black mambas are the world's fastest snakes. They have been timed at 7 miles an hour. In short bursts of speed, they may reach 15 miles an hour—faster than many people can run. Two drops of black mamba poison can kill a grown man within ten minutes.

Black mamba © NEW YORK ZOOLOGICAL SOCIETY

A tangle of young taipans
AUSTRALIAN INFORMATION SERVICE

Australia has more poisonous snakes than harmless ones. There are sixty-three kinds of poisonous snakes in Australia, all members of the cobra family. Some are too small to be dangerous, but others are as deadly as any snake on earth.

The 11-foot taipan (TIE-pan) is Australia's biggest snake. It has been called the most ferocious snake in the world. When it strikes, it bites again and again. Few people recover from a taipan's bite unless they are treated right away.

The tiger snake of southern Australia is another killer. It can be 8 feet long. Since it is more common than the taipan, it bites people more often. Like many poisonous snakes, it gives birth to living young. It has as many as seventy-two babies at one time.

Tiger snake
© NEW YORK ZOOLOGICAL SOCIETY

The death adder is only about 3 feet long, but it lives up to its name. When it bites, it hangs on and chews to get more poison into the wound. Without fast help from a doctor, a person bitten by a death adder has only a fifty-fifty chance to live.

Death adder
© ZOOLOGICAL SOCIETY OF SAN DIEGO

Sea Snakes

Sea snakes spend their lives in the ocean. Their tails are shaped like paddles, and they wave them back and forth as they cut through the water. Sailors have seen them swimming a thousand miles or more from shore. If they are placed on land, they are helpless. They can only squirm and flop about.

About fifty kinds of sea snakes live in the warm waters of the Indian and Pacific oceans. The biggest ones are about 9 feet long. All sea snakes are poisonous. They use their poison to kill the fish and eels they eat, and against enemies.

Sea snakes never attack people unless they are stepped on or grabbed. They sometimes bite fishermen who are trying to remove the snakes from their nets. They have also bitten swimmers who were wading in shallow water, but this does not happen often. Compared to land snakes, sea snakes cause very few human deaths.

Common banded sea snake.
Note the paddle-shaped tail.
© NEW YORK ZOOLOGICAL SOCIETY

True Vipers

Vipers have thick bodies and big heads shaped like wedges. They are the only poisonous snakes with fangs that fold. When a viper closes its jaws, its fangs fold back against the roof of its mouth. When it opens its jaws to strike, the fangs snap forward and are ready for biting.

There are 180 different kinds of vipers. Those called the true vipers live in Europe, Africa, and Asia.

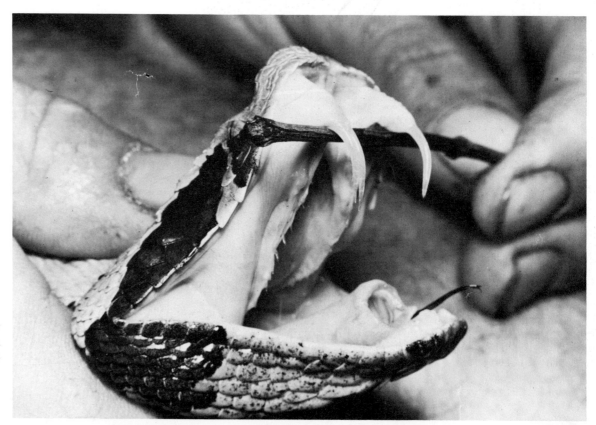

Fangs of a gaboon viper
EDWARD S. ROSS/CALIFORNIA
ACADEMY OF SCIENCES

The 6-foot gaboon viper of Africa is the biggest snake among the true vipers. It has a body as thick as a man's arm and a head the size of a saucer. And it has the longest fangs of any snake. In a large gaboon viper, the fangs are nearly 2 inches long. A gaboon viper can bite through a person's foot. Even so, it is a timid snake that tries to stay away from people.

Gaboon viper

The puff adder probably kills more people in Africa than any other snake. Puff adders are 3 or 4 feet long. During the day they lie hidden in sand or grass. At night they come out to prowl for rats, mice, and birds. Sometimes they chase rats and mice right into people's houses. The puff adder gets its name from the loud puffing sound it makes when disturbed.

Puff adder EDWARD S. ROSS/CALIFORNIA ACADEMY OF SCIENCES

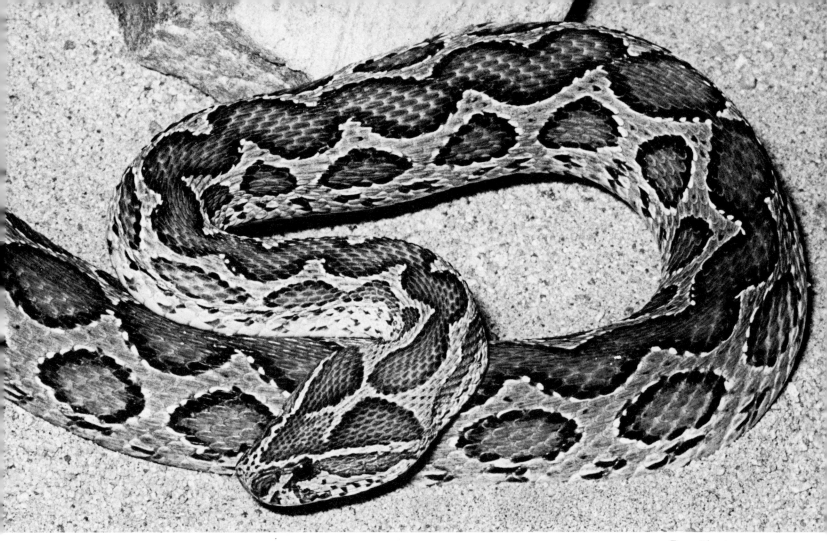

Russell's viper
SY OSKEROFF/
LOS ANGELES ZOO

Russell's viper is a common snake in Asia. In India, it is as feared as the cobra. It also hunts at night, lurking near footpaths and roadways. Like the puff adder, it is not shy about crawling into village houses. People have stepped on these snakes in the dark. The female gives birth to as many as sixty living young. Each baby viper starts life with enough poison to kill four mice.

Pit Vipers

Pit vipers are named for the pits on their cheeks. These pits can sense heat. They tell the snake when a warm-blooded animal is nearby. A pit viper is guided by its pits when it hunts at night. It can strike at its warm-blooded prey in total darkness.

Some pit vipers live in Asia, but most of them are found in North and South America. They include rattlesnakes, copperheads, and cottonmouths.

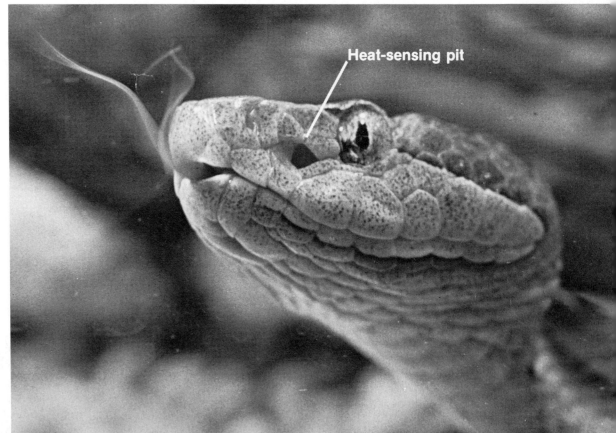

Heat-sensing pit

Copperhead
MAX HIRSHFELD/OFFICE OF
GRAPHICS AND EXHIBITS,
NATIONAL ZOOLOGICAL PARK,
SMITHSONIAN INSTITUTION

The biggest pit viper in the Americas is the bushmaster. It can be 10 feet long. It lives in the tropical forests of South America and the West Indies. Its spotted body is hard to see among the dead leaves of the forest floor. Because of its size, the bushmaster is greatly feared. Actually, it is a shy and sluggish snake that seldom attacks people. Since it stays hidden in the forest, it rarely even sees a person.

Bushmaster hiding among dead leaves. Can you see it?

The fer-de-lance, or lance head, is the most dangerous snake in Central and South America. It reaches a length of 8 feet. Like most pit vipers, it is a silent night hunter. It waits in its lair until twilight. Then it glides along, flicking out its forked tongue. When it finds a good hunting spot, it coils up and waits for a small animal to come within reach.

The fer-de-lance lives both in fields and forests. It is often found on sugar plantations, where it kills large numbers of rats. It also bites barefoot farm workers as they gather sugar cane. Because there are so many of these snakes, they attack people often. They probably cause more deaths in South America than any other snake.

Poisonous Snakes of the United States

Coral snakes are small cousins of the cobras. They're the only members of the cobra family found in the Americas. Two kinds of coral snakes live in the United States. The eastern coral snake is about 3 feet long. It lives in the Southeast, from North Carolina to Texas. The western coral snake is less than 2 feet long. It is found only in Arizona and New Mexico.

Few people ever see a coral snake in the wild. They burrow in fields and hide under old boards and rotting logs. They bite only when they are stepped on or touched. Since they have tiny fangs, they must hold on and chew to work their poison into the wound.

Some people believe that no one can survive a coral snake's bite, but that's not true. Since coral snakes are small, they deliver only a small amount of their poison. Most of the people they bite live to tell about it.

Eastern coral snake
© ZOOLOGICAL SOCIETY
OF SAN DIEGO

Four copperheads
© ZOOLOGICAL SOCIETY
OF SAN DIEGO

Copperheads and cottonmouths are pit vipers. The copperhead is found in many eastern and southern states, especially in woods and among rocks. It ranges as far west as Kansas, Oklahoma, and Texas. It probably bites more people than any other snake in North America. A copperhead bite is painful and must be treated right away. Its poison, however, is rarely strong enough to kill. The biggest copperheads are about 4 feet long.

The cottonmouth, or water moccasin, is bigger than the copperhead. It is also much more poisonous. It lives near lakes, swamps, and streams in the Southeast. Although it doesn't attack people often, its bite can be deadly. Cottonmouths reach a length of about 6 feet. They get their name from the white lining of their mouth and throat.

Cottonmouth E. A. GOLDMAN/U.S. FISH AND WILDLIFE SERVICE

The United States has fifteen different kinds of rattlesnakes. Like copperheads and cottonmouths, they are pit vipers. Rattlers are found in every state but are most common in the Far West. Arizona is the rattlesnake capital of the world. It has eleven kinds of rattlers.

In size, rattlesnakes range from midgets less than 2 feet long to giants about 8 feet long. All rattlesnakes except the smallest can kill a person.

The rattle is a warning signal. It is the rattler's first line of defense. By shaking its tail, a rattler warns away enemies that might attack it or step on it. It does not always rattle, however. If taken by surprise, it may strike without warning.

A rattler can strike about one-third the length of its body. A person must be quite close to be in danger. As the snake lunges forward, its mouth springs open. Its long fangs snap forward and lock in place. After stabbing its victim, the snake pulls back and returns quickly to a coiled position. The entire attack takes about one second.

Rattlesnake skull (left), copperhead skull (right) © NEW YORK ZOOLOGICAL SOCIETY

Timber rattlesnake. It reaches a length of about 6 feet.
JESSIE COHEN/OFFICE OF
GRAPHICS AND EXHIBITS,
NATIONAL ZOOLOGICAL PARK,
SMITHSONIAN INSTITUTION

Western diamondback rattlesnake with newly born young
© NEW YORK ZOOLOGICAL SOCIET[Y]

The biggest and most dangerous rattlesnakes are the eastern and western diamondbacks. When a big diamondback strikes, its poison can kill a mouse within seconds and a grown man within an hour. The eastern diamondback lives in the Southeast, from North Carolina to Louisiana. It can be 8 feet long. It looks even bigger because of its thick body. The western diamondback lives in the Southwest and Mexico. It reaches a length of 7½ feet. It causes more deaths in the United States than any other snake.

36

This is the deadliest snake in North America, a Mojave (moe-HAH-vee) rattlesnake. It looks like a diamondback, but it is much more poisonous. Drop for drop, its poison is at least eight times as strong as any other rattlesnake's. Mojave rattlesnakes are between 2 and 4 feet long. They are found only in desert areas of the Southwest and Mexico.

Mojave rattlesnake
© NEW YORK ZOOLOGICAL SOCIETY

Rattlesnakes eat many kinds of small animals, including rats, mice, gophers, squirrels, chipmunks, and rabbits. Sometimes they catch birds. If they live near streams or lakes, they prey on frogs and toads. Small rattlesnakes often eat lizards. In the wild, rattlers probably eat about once every week or ten days.

Rattlesnakes are killed and eaten in turn by coyotes, foxes, wildcats, and badgers, by dogs, cats, and pigs, by hawks and eagles, and by other snakes, including king snakes, racers, and whip snakes. They have other enemies, too. Many hoofed animals attack rattlers on sight. Deer, sheep, horses, and cattle will try to stamp on any rattler that is caught out in the open.

Like all poisonous snakes, rattlers need their poison to capture food. They try to avoid their enemies by staying out of sight. A rattler will not attack unless it is stepped on, touched, cornered, or surprised. It will never fight if it can get away. When given a chance, it will escape as fast as it can. People may fear poisonous snakes, but the snakes, it seems, are just as afraid of people.

Eastern diamondback rattlesnake.
A snake's forked tongue is harmless.
It picks up odors from the air and
ground. Pit vipers use their tongues
to trail poisoned prey.
© NEW YORK ZOOLOGICAL SOCIETY

Index